MARS.

RUSSIA

CRETE

EGYPT

FRANCE

EIRE

SIERRA LEONE

BRAZIL

IRAQ

NIGERIA

CZECH
REPUBLIC

THAILAND

GREECE

GERMANY.

CANADA.

POLAND

USA
D.

# Olanna's Big Day

Natasha Mac a'Bháird

Illustrated by
Ray Forkan of The Cartoon Saloon

THE O'BRIEN PRESS
DUBLIN

*Dedication*

For Rachel and Sarah

NATASHA MAC A'BHÁIRD combines freelance writing and editing with looking after her twin girls. She is also the author of *The Irish Bride's Survival Guide*.

First published 2009 by The O'Brien Press Ltd,
12 Terenure Road East, Rathgar, Dublin 6, Ireland.
Tel: +353 1 4923333; Fax: +353 1 4922777
E-mail: books@obrien.ie
Website: www.obrien.ie

ISBN: 978-1-84717-171-9

Kindly supported by

The Department of
**Arts, Sport and Tourism**
An Roinn
**Ealaíon, Spóirt agus Turasóireachta**

British Library Cataloguing-in-Publication Data
A catalogue record for this title is available from the British Library

1 2 3 4 5 6 7 8 9 10
09 10 11 12 13

Printed and bound in Poland by Białostockie Zakłady Graficzne S.A.
The paper in this book is produced using pulp from managed forests.

The postman who came to Olanna's house early every morning was called Paddy. Olanna loved to look out for Paddy and see what he had brought.

Sometimes he brought boring letters, with Mama or Papa's name typed on the front.

Sometimes he brought lovely colourful postcards from Olanna's uncle, who was travelling around the world.

Best of all were the parcels from Mama-Bayo, all the way from Nigeria. Mama-Bayo was Olanna's granny. Olanna was sad that Mama-Bayo lived so far away. When she got parcels from her it made her feel closer.

Olanna would bring the stamps into school
and Ms Carr, her teacher, would stick any new ones
onto the big map of the world that hung by the window.

4

Mama-Bayo often sent something she had knitted for Olanna, like a warm cardigan, or a blanket. She sent a lot of scarves, too. Mama said that Mama-Bayo was worried about the cold weather in Ireland and wanted Olanna to be nice and warm.

Olanna loved her scarves: the orange and blue one, the pink and purple one, and the one with all the colours of the rainbow. But her favourite was the long green and white scarf. Mama-Bayo had made it in the colours of the Nigerian flag, and it was just like the one Papa wore to football matches.

Paddy the postman always gave Olanna an extra big smile when he brought a parcel.

'Special delivery from Nigeria!' he would say. 'Now don't eat it all at once – especially if it's another scarf'. Then he would wink and climb back on his bicycle.

Every Friday Olanna had band practice. She played the
tin whistle in the school band. So did Ciara, who sat next
to her in class.

'Stop chattering, everyone!' called the band leader. 'Line
up in your places. All together now, keep in step!'

Round and round the hall they marched. The trumpets
tooted loudly, and the flutes played softly. **Bang, bang**
went the drum.

When practice was over, the children ran to put away their instruments. Olanna kept her tin whistle in her schoolbag. Tommy didn't because he played the drum. Olanna didn't think you could get a schoolbag big enough to carry a drum.

Tommy looked so funny carrying the drum. It was nearly as big as himself, with a special strap that went over his shoulder and around his back. But when he started playing he didn't look funny any more. He looked really cool.

Olanna didn't like to stand too close to him when he was playing the drum. It made her want to put her hands over her ears, which is difficult to do when you are playing the tin whistle.

They were getting ready to leave when the band leader clapped her hands together for attention. 'Boys and girls, I have some exciting news. We are going to march in the Saint Patrick's Day parade in two weeks. So we need to practise very hard to make sure everything is perfect.'

There was a buzz of excitement around the hall.

'What's Saint Patrick's Day?' Olanna whispered to Ciara.

'You know, Paddy's Day!' said Ciara.

Paddy the postman had a special day? Olanna had never heard of this. Maybe it was a custom in Ireland. In Nigeria, postmen didn't get a special day to themselves, she told Ciara.

'No, silly,' Ciara laughed. 'Not Paddy the postman. *Saint Patrick* – he's Ireland's special saint. We don't have to go to school on his feast day and there's a huge parade, with floats, and dragons, and all kinds of puppets.'

'And girls dancing, and pipe bands playing,' added Stefan.

'And US!' said Tommy.

'And you can eat all the sweets you want,' Ciara said.
'I'm saving mine up, I'm going to eat at least four
packets!'

'I'm going to eat five bars of chocolate,' Tommy said.

'And everyone wears green, and your mum puts
shamrock on your clothes,' Ciara said.

Olanna thought it sounded a bit like Independence Day
in Nigeria, when there were parades and everyone
celebrated together.

All the boys and girls practised their tunes to get ready for the parade. Olanna and Ciara met in the schoolyard at break time to practise the tin whistle together.

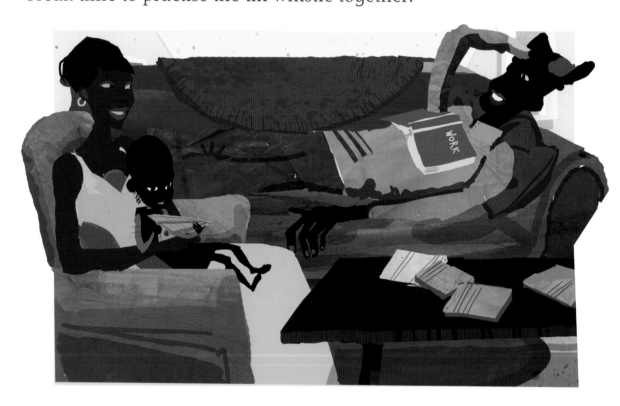

Olanna told her parents about Saint Patrick's Day. It was a holiday for everyone. Papa wouldn't have to go to work, he could come to watch Olanna in the parade. Olanna wished Mama-Bayo could come too, but it was too far for her to travel.

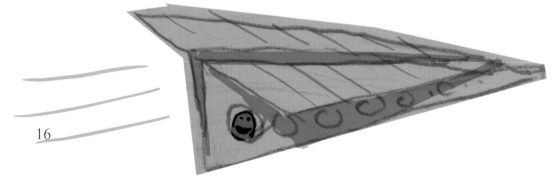

At last the special day was here! Mama ironed Olanna's band uniform and put ribbons in her hair.

Papa bought some shamrock and pinned it on Olanna's uniform. He pinned a big bunch on his coat and on Mama's new dress. They were ready to go!

As they were leaving, Olanna grabbed her green and white scarf and wrapped it around her neck. She hoped the band leader wouldn't notice. They weren't supposed to wear scarves with their uniforms, but Olanna wanted Mama-Bayo to be part of the parade too.

The band met in the car park near the church. The sun was shining but it was a cold day. The children stamped their feet to keep warm.

Ciara noticed Olanna's green and white scarf.

'Did your granny knit that scarf for Saint Patrick's Day?' she asked.

'Not really. Green and white are the Nigerian colours,' Olanna told her. 'But they're the right colours for Saint Patrick's Day too!'

Nearby some of the other performers were getting ready. There were girls in Irish dancing costumes, their ringlets bouncing as they practised their steps.

There were men wearing kilts and carrying strange-looking instruments.

'They're bagpipes,' Tommy explained. 'You have to blow into them very hard and they make a strange noise – like cats!'

Men in shiny costumes walked on stilts and tried not to bump into the leprechauns who were leaping around.

A huge dragon waved its long green and yellow tail.

The band got into their places behind Tommy and his
big drum. Olanna felt nervous, but excited too.

Then suddenly, disaster! The strap holding Tommy's
drum broke and the drum fell onto the ground! The band
leader stuck out her foot just in time to stop it rolling down
the road.

What were they going to do now? The drum was the
most important instrument in the band. How could they
march without it?

The parade was about to start! There was no time to fix the strap. Tommy looked like he was going to burst into tears.

Then Olanna had an idea. 'My scarf!' she said. 'We can use my scarf instead of a strap!'

'Great idea, Olanna!' said the band leader. She took Olanna's scarf and tied it onto the drum, then helped put it over Tommy's head and settled it around his shoulder.

It worked! All the boys and girls cheered.

'Quickly, everyone, back to your places!' said the band leader.

Tommy began banging the drum, their signal to move off.

Olanna marched proudly behind Tommy, playing her tin whistle.

When the parade passed by Mama and Papa, Olanna saw them cheering and waving.

The band was a great success.

Olanna couldn't wait to get home to ring Mama-Bayo.

She told her all about the parade and how Mama-Bayo's green and white scarf had

## SAVED THE DAY!